Read more classic books from the Devlins!

Cranberry Thanksgiving
Cranberry Christmas
Cranberry Valentine
Old Black Witch!
Old Witch and the Polka-Dot Ribbon

CRANBERRY HALLOWEEN

WENDE and HARRY DEVLIN

Purple House Press   Kentucky

Published by Purple House Press
an imprint of Purple House, Inc.
PO Box 787, Cynthiana, KY 41031

ISBN13 978-1-930900-69-1   LCCN 2013941650

Summary: On Halloween night the people of Cranberryport almost lose the
money they have raised to build a new dock.

Find more classic books for kids at
www.purplehousepress.com

Printed in South Korea by PACOM
1 2 3 4 5 6 7 8 9 10
First Edition

For our grandson, Bryan Monteith Gates

The New England October skies were bright and blue. Orange and yellow pumpkins lay in the fields and the smell of cider was everywhere.

"Halloween! Wonderful Halloween is coming," said Maggie, throwing her hat in the air.

Grandmother stopped stirring her cake. "Halloween *is* coming but there will be two weeks of hard work before it does. All the money for the new dock must be in on Halloween night or it can't be finished by winter."

A week ago, when the Cranberryport dock had been swept away by a wild storm, the townspeople had gathered in dismay at their Town Hall.

What would Cranberryport be without a dock?

Where would they tie their boats?

Where would the children gather to fish and swim?

Where would they all meet to picnic and watch sunsets?

"We will build a *new* dock," said the mayor.

"And we will all help to raise the money," said Grandmother.

"Suffering codfish! I'll collect the money," said Mr. Whiskers. "I have my grandfather's moneybox."

"Then you shall be treasurer, Mr. Whiskers," said the mayor.

"And I'll guard your blinking money with my life," said the old clamdigger, saluting proudly.

But not everyone wanted Mr. Whiskers to be treasurer. Mr. Grape was not about to let his least favorite neighbor enjoy such an honor.

"I object," said Mr. Grape. He banged his cane on the floor. "I *double* object. Mr. Whiskers doesn't pull his weeds, doesn't paint his house, and doesn't wash his windows. He'll lose your money."

Grandmother stood and looked Mr. Grape in the eye. "Mr. Whiskers would never let his friends down."

The crowd quite agreed with Grandmother and Mr. Grape left, shaking his cane angrily.

The people of Cranberryport went home and began to plan how they would earn money. Everyone wanted to help. Grandmother and her friends would have pie and cake sales. Maggie would sell old books. Mr. Whiskers began to gather clams to make chowder to sell at the general store.

One day Mr. Whiskers walked up the long path to Mr. Grape's big brick house on the hill to ask for a donation. He waved to Mr. Grape's two redheaded gardeners and rang the front doorbell.

Mr. Grape jumped in rage when he saw Mr. Whiskers.

"Never! I'll give no money for your dock — you whiskery humbug — and stay away from my house!"

Mr. Whiskers forgot all his good intentions. "Why you old scoundrel! Where's your town pride?"

Mr. Grape slammed his door. Grumbling and growling, Mr. Whiskers made his way back over the cranberry bogs to his tiny, gray cottage on the beach.

The night of Halloween finally arrived, cold and moonlit.

Tonight all the money would be counted at Town Hall and a wonderful party would follow with cider and doughnuts for all.

Grandmother packed her basket with sugar doughnuts and went ahead to prepare for the party.

Later, Mr. Whiskers stopped by to walk Maggie into town.

Maggie wore a pink and green clown costume with a pointed clown's hat. Mr. Whiskers, dressed as a ghost, tapped his moneybox proudly. "Almost full," he boasted to Maggie.

They started for town. The rising winds in the pines and the screech of an owl were the only sounds in the blue night. A dark, empty house, next to a bridge loomed against the sky.

"Do we have to pass by that house tonight?" asked Maggie.

"It's not so bad. I played in it when I was a boy," said Mr. Whiskers. "My old Aunt Pru lived there."

Suddenly Maggie whispered, "Stop! I hear someone behind us."

Mr. Whiskers whirled to see two burly men in pirate costumes almost upon them.

"Hand over that moneybox," one of them hissed.

"Mind your blinking manners," roared Mr. Whiskers. "Nobody takes *my* moneybox." He grabbed Maggie's hand and ran up the vine-tangled path to the deserted house.

The dark of the night and heavy boots slowed the pursuing pirates.

Running like the wind, Maggie and Mr. Whiskers fled to the front door. They pulled it open and squeezed in. Panting, Mr. Whiskers locked the door behind.

"Run for the back door and lock it," shouted Mr. Whiskers. Maggie felt her way through the darkened house, found the kitchen door, and bolted it — just in time! For in the window she saw the fierce mask of one of the pirates. He pounded on the door and shouted, "Open up — we have you trapped."

Mr. Whiskers and Maggie, their hearts beating wildly, leaned against the kitchen wall and listened. The old house was filled with noises. Upstairs the doors creaked, the wind moaned through the turrets, and shutters banged.

"I think I don't believe in ghosts," said Mr. Whiskers uneasily.

"I think I don't either," echoed Maggie.

"Good," said Mr. Whiskers. "Let's find a way out of here."

Mr. Whiskers looked all around the kitchen. "Maggie, I remember something. We used to come in from the springhouse by an underground passageway. Are you game to go down to the cellar?"

Maggie thought of spiders, mice, and damp darkness, but with sudden spirit, she said, "Let's go!"

Mr. Whiskers led the way. At the foot of the squeaking cellar stairs, he struck a match. The dim light showed a rough, mossy door. Mr. Whiskers put his shoulder to the door and heaved mightily. An ancient bolt snapped and the door swung away as mice scuttled and spiders scattered into the darkness.

Mr. Whiskers fought his way through cobwebs. Maggie followed, clutching Mr. Whiskers' sheet. Stumbling and groping through the underground passageway they came, in time, to the springhouse. At last, Mr. Whiskers and Maggie pushed their way into the clear night air.

"Shhh," whispered Mr. Whiskers. "We can slip away behind these pine trees." Silently, they crept from the house, back to the road, and then off to town.

At Town Hall, Grandmother worried and fussed, the mayor fumed, and the rest of the party became impatient at the absence of Mr. Whiskers and Maggie.

The children had paraded around in their costumes. A feast of homemade doughnuts and pitchers of golden cider was placed on the tables.

Everyone was anxious to eat, but where were Mr. Whiskers and Maggie? And where was Cranberryport's money?

Mr. Grape jumped to his feet. He looked very pleased.

"You wouldn't listen to me. I told you Mr. Whiskers couldn't be trusted. You won't see that old good-for-nothing tonight!"

While Mr. Grape scolded the mayor and the crowd, a ghost and a small clown slipped into the midst of the party. After whispering to the sheriff, the ghost made his way through the crowd to Mr. Grape.

In a sudden flurry, the ghost threw off his sheet and there Mr. Whiskers stood in a grinning triumph.

"Well, suffering codfish! I'm here — and so is my moneybox!" said Mr. Whiskers.

Mr. Grape gawked and gasped and fell back in his chair. "You have the moneybox?" he squeaked anxiously.

Behind the crowd, the sheriff's voice boomed. He held two pirates in tow. "It's just at Mr. Whiskers said. These two rascals thought they had Mr. Whiskers and Maggie trapped in the old Peabody house."

Mr. Whiskers stared at the unmasked pirates.

"Why, they are Mr. Grape's gardeners!" he said in amazement.

"He's the one who made us do it," said the gardeners, pointing to Mr. Grape.

Mr. Grape began to tiptoe toward the door when the sheriff's voice rang out. "Sit right here until I decide what to do with you, sir."

Now the mayor, who had been counting the money for the new dock, rose to his feet and faced the crowd. "Bad news," he said. "There just isn't enough money for the new dock."

The crowd groaned.

Mr. Grape raised his hand. "Would you allow this public-spirited citizen to make up the difference?" He looked in the sheriff's direction with what he hoped was a winning smile.

The sheriff turned to Mr. Whiskers. "Well, it's up to you, sir."

Mr. Whiskers took a bite of doughnut, brushed the sugar from his brass-buttoned coat, and hummed a little tune.

Slowly, he smiled through his whiskers and said, "For the folks of Cranberryport we might accept that blinking offer."

The sheriff took his hand from Mr. Grape's shoulder and turned to the pirates. "And you two had better tend to your gardening."

Mr. Grape sighed with relief.

The rest of the evening was a Halloween celebration. Cranberryport would have a new dock and everyone delighted in bobbing for apples, singing, and drinking cider.

"You were a fine treasurer," said Grandmother as she watched Mr. Whiskers bob for apples.

"Yes, I'm a blooming wonder," said Mr. Whiskers.

Maggie laughed.

Grandmother shook her head.

And Mr. Whiskers went down in the tub again in a final try for the apple.

Cranberry Dessert

4 cups ground or chopped cranberries
2 cups sugar
1 cup drained, cubed pineapple
1 cup chopped nuts
1½ cups miniature marshmallows
2 envelopes jello, or one large lemon-flavored
    jello, dissolved in ½ cup water

Combine ingredients. Quickly fold in 2 cups whipped topping. Allow to set in refrigerator until firm.

Simpler Version

4 cups ground or chopped cranberries
1½ cups sugar
1 cup drained, cubed pineapple
1 cup chopped nuts
1½ cups miniature marshmallows
2 cups whipped topping

Combine ingredients and serve in dessert glasses.